The Problem with Pumpkins

A Hip & Hop Story

BARNEY SALTZBERG

GULLIVER BOOKS
HARCOURT, INC.
San Diego   New York   London

Requests for permission to make copies of any part of the work
should be mailed to the following address:
Permissions Department, Harcourt, Inc.,
6277 Sea Harbor Drive, Orlando, Florida 32887-6777.

www.harcourt.com

Gulliver Books is a trademark of Harcourt, Inc.,
registered in the United States of America and/or other jurisdictions.

Library of Congress Cataloging-in-Publication Data
Saltzberg, Barney.
The problem with pumpkins: a Hip and Hop story/Barney Saltzberg.
p.   cm.
"Gulliver Books."
Summary: Hip and Hop's friendship is tested when Hop insists they
can't both be pumpkins for Halloween.
[1. Halloween—Fiction.   2. Costume—Fiction.
3. Best friends—Fiction.]   I. Title.
PZ7.S1552Pr   2001
[E]—dc21   00-11540
ISBN 0-15-202489-1

First edition
A C E G H F D B

Printed in Singapore

The illustrations in this book were done in pen-and-ink,
Dr. Martin's Watercolors, and Prisma colored pencils.
The display type was set in Boink.
The text type was set in Souvenir.
Color separations by Bright Arts Ltd., Hong Kong
Printed and bound by Tien Wah Press, Singapore
This book was printed on totally chlorine-free Nymolla Matte Art paper.
Production supervision by Sandra Grebenar and Ginger Boyer
Designed by Ivan Holmes

For Billy & Nibbly & Noop & Goodink

CHAPTER ONE

A week before Halloween, Hip and Hop went to buy
supplies to make their costumes.

"I can't wait for Halloween," said Hop. "I'm going to be a
pumpkin."

"I'm going to be a pumpkin, too!" said Hip.

"I said it first!" said Hop. "You have to pick something else."

"But I really want to be a pumpkin!" said Hip.

"Too bad," said Hop.

"That's not fair," grumbled Hip.

At the store, Hop bought orange satin, green felt, and black paint.

"Hip," said Hop, "shouldn't you be buying supplies, too?"

"I want to be a pumpkin!" said Hip. "Pumpkins are perfect. They're round. They're orange. They're Halloweeny... And that's what I want to be."

"You could be a bat," said Hop. "Bats are Halloweeny."

"I don't like bats," said Hip.

"What about a witch?" said Hop. "Witches are very Halloweeny."

"No!" said Hip. "I was a witch last year. I want to be a pumpkin."

"How about a pirate?" said Hop. "If you're a pirate, I'll give you *every* green M&M I get from trick-or-treating."

"I love green M&M's!" said Hip. "OK, if you give me all the green M&M's *and* I get to pick *both* of our costumes for next year."

"Deal!" said Hop.

"Why are you buying the same things as me?" asked Hop.
"Because I'm going to be an orange-and-green pirate with a black beard," said Hip.

Back at his house, Hop crunched old newspapers to
stuff his pumpkin suit. Hip crunched old newspapers, too.
"Stop copying me," said Hop.
"I'm not," said Hip. "Pirates have *big* bellies."

Hop sewed an orange satin pumpkin body and painted a
big, smiling jack-o'-lantern face on the front.

Hip practiced painting her beard.

Hop made a green-felt stem hat for his costume.

"I wish I had a hat like that," said Hip.

"Pirates don't wear hats like this," said Hop.

"I know," said Hip. "Only pumpkins are lucky enough to have nice little green hats like the one you're going to wear and I'm not."

Hip practiced being a pirate.

"Reading would be much easier if I were a pumpkin," she said, sighing.

"You can be a pumpkin next year," said Hop. "This year
you get all the green M&M's. Remember?"
"How could I forget!" said Hip.

CHAPTER TWO

On Halloween day, Hip and Hop decorated their houses.
"Does that cloud look like a pumpkin to you?" asked Hip.
"No," said Hop. "It looks like a storm is coming!"

"Oh no. I think I heard thunder!" said Hop.
"Well, maybe it won't rain," said Hip.

"It *is* raining!" cried Hop. "It can't rain on Halloween. Nobody goes trick-or-treating in the rain. Halloween will be a disaster!"

Outside it rained, and inside Hop sulked all afternoon.
Hip hated seeing Hop so upset. Finally she said, "I'll be right
back."

"One whiff of this candy and nobody will care that it's raining," Hip announced. "We'll have trick-or-treaters here in no time!"

Hip and Hop waited, but no one came.

Hip had another idea. She played scary music to attract trick-or-treaters.

"Well, this would have worked if the thunder wasn't making so much noise," said Hip.

"Nobody's coming," groaned Hop. "I told you Halloween would be a disaster!"

Hip ran back home.

A few minutes later, a ghost knocked on Hop's door.

Hop smiled for the first time all afternoon. "Haven't I seen you before?"

"Of course . . . I mean, no . . . I mean, boo!" said the ghost.

"Look, the rain stopped!" shouted Hop.

"Hey, Hip," said Hop, "let's leave the candy in a bowl by the door and go trick-or-treating ourselves!"

"Great idea," said Hip. "But how did you know it was me?"

"You're my best friend," said Hop. "Besides, I know what your sheets look like!"

CHAPTER THREE

Hop put on his pumpkin suit and his pumpkin hat.

"Did I mention that I, Hip, your best friend, would really rather be a pumpkin more than anything else in the whole wide world?" asked Hip.

"Yes," said Hop, "but *I'm* going to be the pumpkin, and *you're* going to get all my green M&M's."

"Fine!" grumbled Hip.

Hip put on her pirate costume.
"I look terrible!" she groaned.

"I bet it would help if you put on your eye patch,"
suggested Hop.
But they couldn't find it anywhere.

"It's OK," said Hip. "I don't want to be a pirate, anyway."
"But, Hip," cried Hop, "you've been practicing to be a pirate all week!"

"But I never really *wanted* to be a pirate," said Hip.

"Wait, wait, wait!" said Hop. "There *must* be something else you could be..."

"I could draw windows on this box, and you could be a skyscraper," Hop said.

"It's too stuffy in here," said Hip.

"You could be a red snapper fish. All you have to do is wear red, and snap your fingers," suggested Hop.

"I don't know how to snap my fingers," said Hip.

"We could paint these egg cartons green, and you could
be an alligator," said Hop.

"No," said Hip. "I want to be a *pumpkin*! It's the only
thing I want to be."

"But *I'm* the pumpkin," said Hop.

"Well, you're not my boss. If I can't be a pumpkin, I'm going home. You can trick-or-treat by yourself!" said Hip.

Hip stomped home and flopped on the floor. *This is the worst Halloween I've ever had!* she thought. *I don't get to be a pumpkin, and now I'm not even going to get any green M&M's.*

After a little while, Hip heard a knock at her door. "I'm terribly sorry!" she called. "I don't have any candy. I'm not supposed to be here. I really should be out trick-or-treating..."

"It's me. I'm not here for the candy," Hop said. "I'd rather
we were both pumpkins, than trick-or-treat all by myself."

Hop pushed open the door all the way, and there, sitting on the front step, was a big pumpkin suit.

"It's for you!" said Hop.

Hip tried on the costume.

"It's pretty nice!" she said. "But I thought we weren't supposed to wear the same thing."

"We're not," Hop told her. "My costume is smaller than yours. Yours is bigger than mine. My pumpkin's face is happy. Your pumpkin's face is scary!"

"Now that I'm a pumpkin," said Hip, "can I still get all of your green M&M's and pick our costumes for next year?"

"Sure," said Hop. "I'm glad we're trick-or-treating together!"

"Me, too," said Hip. "I was thinking . . . all of those green M&M's might get lonely being away from the other colors. Do you think I could have all of your red M&M's, too? Just to make the green ones happy!"

"Of course," said Hop. "There's nothing worse than lonely candy!"